I0526914

"Just as butterflies, humans are beautiful too, no matter how an individual's outer appearance may look in the eyes of others. It is the beauty within themselves that make them blossom into beautiful butterflies."

-*Sandra Barnes*

Special Dedication

"To my wonderful grandchildren *A'niya* and *Stephon*."

Reflection
of a
Broken Butterfly

ASA PUBLISHING CORPORATION
AN INNOVATIVE OUTSOURCE BOOK PUBLISHING HYBRID

ASA Publishing Corporation
An Accredited Hybrid Publishing House with the BBB
www.asapublishingcorporation.com

1285 N. Telegraph Rd., 376, Monroe, Michigan 48162

All Rights Reserved. No part of this publication may be reproduced, stored in a retrieval system or transmitted in any form or by any means electronic, mechanical, photocopying, recording or otherwise, without the prior written permission of the publisher. Author/writer rights to "Freedom of Speech" protected by and with the "1st Amendment" of the Constitution of the United States of America. This is a work of fiction. Any resemblance to actual events, locales, person living or deceased that is not related to the author's literacy is entirely coincidental.

With this title/copyright page, the reader is notified that the publisher does not assume, and expressly disclaims any obligation to obtain and/or include any other information other than that provided by the author except with permission. Any belief system, promotional motivations, including but not limited to the use of non-fictional/fictional characters and/or characteristics of this book, are within the boundaries of the author's own creativity in order to reflect the nature and concept of the book.

Any and all vending sales and distribution not permitted without full book cover and this copyright page.

Copyrights©2018, 2019 Sandra Barnes, (Realistic Writing Incorporation LLC) All Rights Reserved
Book Title: Reflection of a Broken Butterfly
Date Published: 12.2018 / 04.25.2019
Edition: 1, *Trade Paperback*
Book ID: ASAPCID2380777
ISBN: 978-1-946746-46-7
LCCN: 2019940020

This book was published in the United States of America.
Great State of Michigan

Reflection
of a
Broken Butterfly

SANDRA BARNES

Once upon a time there was a baby caterpillar named Pendora who had just been born and began exploring the world.

As Pendora got older, she would enjoy watching all the wonderful butterflies flying around and hoped that one day she can be as beautiful as them.

Now it was time for her caterpillar cycle to end, and Pendora started forming her own little silky cocoon, waiting for the day to soar the air like the others.

One day while being sheltered and protected from the outside world there were a few caterpillars passing by. As they looked up she could hear them say to each other, "That is an ugly little cocoon."

Hearing those words she began to think to herself, "If my cocoon is ugly, I wonder what I am going to look like when I get out of my home?"

Day after day continuing to hear the talking and the laughter about her cocoon she began to cry. She said to herself, "How much longer am I going to be stuck in here? I really want to see the others."

Through it all Pendora did not become discouraged.

Weeks have passed, Pendora has now been released out of her cocoon. Greeting the outside with a glow of wonder, she began flying around to explore her new world. As Pendora was soaring, she stumbled upon a small pond. Saying to herself with great excitement, "I am going to go a little closer to the water so that I can take a good look at myself."

Reaching the surface of the pond and taking a look at her reflection in the water, she began to cry out loud, saying "Why do I look the way I do?! Why do I have all the wrong colors on my wings?!" Pendora staring at herself for a few more seconds, she began to wonder about the way she looked. Sadly, she then turned and flew away from the pond.

Continuing on her journey she came upon a group of beautiful butterflies, she decided to stop and introduce herself. When she did, they all burst into laughter and began calling her names.

Becoming very sad and broken hearted she quietly flew away

from the crowd. While flying away she began to imagine seeing herself still blossoming into a beautiful butterfly, so that she could show everyone that she can be beautiful too.

As the month passed along, Pendora's colors began changing but they still were not as pretty as she thought they would become. One morning while flying around she noticed a group of butterflies attending school. She thought, "Let me drop in and see if I can meet a few new friends."

Pendora flew into the group of butterflies to join in for a little while. Thinking that it was okay, to her surprise everyone began laughing at the colors of her wings. Again, becoming very heartbroken she flew away to her home. Still feeling ugly and unwanted she packed her things to go far, far away. When Pendora finished, she took off in flight to find herself a new home.

Pendora was starting out on her new adventure. She began flying and flying until she became very tired. Needing to rest she stopped in a little city with nothing but all beautiful butterflies. For a better view she landed on a tiny tree branch overlooking the city.

Thinking that she was going to enjoy the scenery alone she heard a voice saying to her, "May I join you for the view?" asked the voice, paying no attention to her wings.

She then turned and looked at where it came from. Really not knowing what to say she said, "Sure you can join me."

The little butterfly said to her, "My name is Smurk and you are?"

Surprised he had asked, she turned and said to him, "My name is Pendora and I am so happy to meet you!"

Smurk then asked, "Would you like to be my friend?"

Smiling, she looked at him and responded, "But you don't mind the color of my wings?"

He said to her, "I see nothing wrong with your wings."

Pendora said to herself, "*Finally I have a friend.*"

But what Pendora did not know was that he did not have any friends either. After enjoying the view together, they both went their separate ways.

The following day Pendora returned to the tree. As she is sitting there watching all the beautiful butterflies flying around and having fun, Smurk appeared and sat beside her.

He said, "Come on! Let us go and see the city."

Pendora became very nervous because of the colors of her wings.

Smurk once again said, "Come on! You have nothing to worry about. Let's go."

Taking off in flight, Pendora and Smurk began to fly around the city. While viewing the city of beautiful butterflies, she begins to hear laughter.

Smurk looking around said to her, "Pay them no attention. We are going to have some fun."

Ignoring the other butterflies and continuing to enjoy all the fun Pendora thought she could never have, she over exhausted herself, became very weak, and fell to the ground. Smurk hurried to her rescue.

Being very worried he asked, "Pendora, are you okay?"

She said to him, "I am a little tired from all the flying around the city, and besides, everyone is picking on me."

He said to her, "I understand. I am sorry. Why not just go home and I will see you tomorrow."

The next day Pendora went to look for Smurk, hoping to find him. Pendora did not know that the night before all the other butterflies had been picking on him about flying around the city with her. It made him become ashamed of her, so he had to try to figure out a way to fit in with the crowd.

Minutes later, Smurk arrived but this time he sat far away from his friend Pendora. She pondered for a couple of seconds, then asked him, "Why are you sitting so far away?"

Not wanting to tell Pendora the truth and hurt her feelings, he turned to her and said, "I am sitting here because I am looking for someone."

She then said to Smurk, "Oh, it's okay that you sit over there. I was thinking that you did not want to be with me."

A short while later, a few of the beautiful butterflies came; the ones that were picking on Smurk the night before. Flying up to him they said, "Why are you hanging around with little Miss Ugly?!"

To keep his self-respect he fluttered his wings, giving Pendora a look and flew away leaving her sitting there all alone.

Poor Pendora was sitting there all alone. She realized, "*I have to defend myself once and for all to stop everyone from picking on me.*"

The beautiful butterflies thought that Pendora would fly away. To their surprise Pendora fluttered her wings and shouted, "I am not afraid of you all!!! You can pick on me all you want. Laughing at the color of my wings. Just because you think I am not as beautiful as you are on the outside, the reflection of me on the inside will always be more beautiful than all of you!"

With no more fear Pendora opened her wings, held her head up as high as it could reach, giving a laugh and a great big smile she soared away into the air.

The End

Here are some questions to see if we can identify what Pandora was going through, and if we can also see it happening today!

1. What did you think when the other caterpillars were laughing at Pandora in her cocoon?

2. What was Pandora's reaction to that?

3. Do you think what they did was right or wrong?

4. When the butterflies were teasing and saying that Pandora was ugly, how did you feel hearing it?

5. What kind of behavioral example did those butterflies have?

6. When Pandora met Smurk, how did you think she first felt?

7. What did Smurk and Pandora decide to do on their adventure together?

8. On the very next day, why did Smurk ignore Pandora? What made him act that way?

9. If there was any peer pressure on Smurk, what should or could he have done?

10. What did Pandora decide to do for herself?

11. What did she tell the beautiful butterflies that were being mean to her?

12. Did you learn anything from this story?

Great!

Maybe we can share what being kind to others is all about.

- Never pressure someone to do something that is not right.

- Always be respectful to others.

- And most of all, always learn to love yourself.

- You are your first best friend!

www.ingramcontent.com/pod-product-compliance
Lightning Source LLC
Chambersburg PA
CBHW041006170626
46815CB00002B/182